EVERYTHING

EVERYTHING

Susan Clare Anderson

Rev. date: 01/09/2020

To order additional copies of this book, contact:
Xlibris
1-888-795-4274
www.Xlibris.com
Orders@Xlibris.com
808222

CHAPTER 1

Violet Crystal mine was difficult to reach, but Max and Rick made their way through the rugged mountain terrain of the Arizona desert to find it. Worth 4-6 dollars a carat, the beautiful purple colored Amethyst used to sparkle in between wooden supports designed to protect the miners from the roof and walls collapsing in on them. Sadly, Max looked at Rick waving his flat head screwdriver delicately in the air.

"These veins are tapped out," he half whispered under a dirty red beard. "There's nothing here."

"Yep, I think you're right," agreed Rick through gritty teeth.

"Well," Max continued, letting out a deep sigh, "It's almost time to hike back down the hill to catch our ride back into town. What do you say we grab a bite to eat?"

Rick nodded slowly in agreement. "Yep," he answered, "Let's see what Bradley has for us today." They both forced a smile.

"Looks like cheesy rice again," Bradley declared as he reached for the family sized instant rice package and the jug of water that he labored hard to bring up the hill with him. He heard shouting from outside and lifted up the tent's flap to see what was happening.

"Cave in!!!" someone was yelling. All he could see was a cloud of fine dirt climbing into the sky. When the cloud finally settled, he could see Max crawling out the small opening that once had been the mine's entrance. On his hands and knees, he turned and pulled Rick out of the tight opening.

"I have to get him to town," Max yelled to Bradley. "We'll start down and after you break up camp, follow after us!" Gently, he lifted Rick up. Bradley watched as they staggered down the steep hill together.

Quickly, Bradley turned back to the meal he was preparing and threw handfuls of dirt on the open flame. He realized he had a lot to pack up and not a lot of time to do it in, so he worked fast. Finally, he struggled to tuck the tent into his pack along with the last of the kitchen supplies and took one last look around. Max's tool belt and box of sorted containers to hold the crystals he found would be too awkward to carry with all the kitchen things. So he left them behind. Anxiously, he headed down the narrow path to the riverbed, looking back one last time at the small entrance left in the opening to the mine. Bradley felt very relieved that they both made it out alive. Suddenly the ground gave way beneath him. He landed hard on his side, skidding down the blind hillside, out of control. Desperately, he dug his boot deep into the dirt. He clawed hard at the moving soil, but it buckled up into a trail of gravel chasing him further and further down into the desert. His pants filled with sand, he finally managed to stop in a heap of rocks.

Blinking his eyes, he searched up the hill to see where he was. Taking in quick breaths he carefully tried to stand up, but the ground rolled under his right hand. He clutched at the rocks beneath him, bringing up an egg shaped rock. It glowed briefly under the darkening sky.

"Wait, what the..., a geode!!" he half laughed, recognizing the rock's shape. He tucked it under his arm and crawled slowly back up the hill.

CHAPTER 2

The camp felt eerily quiet since the rest of the crew had left without him. He knew someone would be back for him in the morning when they noticed him missing. Also, he knew not to attempt the climb down in the dark by himself. Tired, he made his way over to where the kitchen tent had been earlier and pitched the tent again. He sat down on a portable chair near the tent's entrance and fumbled the egg shaped rock around in his hands. Sometimes geodes are worth a little money, he thought. He looked around for something sharp to open it with.

Finding a small axe, he broke open the rock, but there were just a few blue and purple strands of crystal, small and disorganized in shape and not worth much. As he stared the small crystals began to straighten. He looked closer and realized he was looking into a very small, tiny face!

Alarmed, he really stiffened when the small crystal person began to speak!

"Hello," the crystal person said.

"Hello," replied Bradley and shaking his head he added, "I'm sorry, but what are you?"

"I'm a Geo Sprite," the tiny person told him.

"A Geo Sprite," Bradley repeated.

"Yes," the Geo Sprite informed him, "When the magnetic fields of the earth are strong their energy can sometimes create a Sprite instead of crystals. I'm one of them. Sprites are very rare and magical. They are allowed to grant one wish to anyone who finds them. The wish has to be made quickly, however, because Geo Sprites don't last long once they are exposed to the earth's atmosphere."

Delighted, Bradley thought for a moment, but didn't know what to wish for. There are so many things he would like, to end hunger, to create world peace, to end disease, or maybe he'd like to have designer tennis shoes? The Sprite began to move slowly and pressed him to hurry with his wish or he wouldn't get one. So, Bradley panicked, and wished for EVERYTHING. The Sprite asked him to repeat his wish and again, Bradley blurted out, "EVERYTHING!"

"Okay," the Sprite said slowly, "You shall have everything."

And then the Sprite was gone with only a few crystal shavings left behind.

Bradley walked outside into the night air. He stumbled over a small tree branch on the ground and as he stepped down, his foot struck something sharp. Picking the object up, he examined it closely. It was a small pocket knife with its blade open. He figured it must belong to Max or Rick and folding it shut, he placed it in his pocket. Then, he waited.

CHAPTER 3

There was no moon that night, Bradley observed. Or maybe the steep slope of the mountain blocked its light out. He waited for what seemed the right amount of time for a wish to come true, but when nothing happened, he gave up and dragged himself back into the tent. He was very sore and tired from his fall down the side of the hill. Remembering the knife in his pocket, he pulled it out and tossed it on an overturned box, next to the empty shell of rock he had found the Sprite in. Sitting down on his portable chair, he wondered if there really are such things as Geo Sprites or if it had all just been his imagination. Without realizing it, his eyes closed and his head drooped slightly to one side. He had fallen to sleep.

He began to dream he was running through the main street of a town he had never seen before, but in the actual dream it was familiar to him and he knew where he was. He saw himself running through the town very fast and over his shoulder he could see many people running with him. They were chasing after him!

He ran until he reached a building with many doors and frantically, he turned the handle on each door. None of them would open. Then, one of the doors opened. He rushed in with the crowd closing in on his heels. Breathing heavily, he closed the door on them and continued to run until he realized he was running between plant vines with a fruit on them that he had never seen before. Turning back, he saw that the door he came in from had vanished and it was now just fields of vines that offered this strange fruit. Cautiously, he picked one of the fruits off its vine and holding it up to the bright sun; he was amazed that he could see right through it. The fruit then disappeared and with a jerk, he yanked his head up and he was back in the tent where he sat on his portable chair.

Puzzled, he stood up and walked over to the knife he had picked up the night before. He looked around and from a hunk of soft wood he found near the tent, he carved a lollipop. His Aunt, who he stayed with when he wasn't out on mining trips, loved lollipops. He thought he would make one and give it to her as a silly surprise. He finished it and balanced it on the thin arm of the chair. A tiny flicker of light next to the corner of his eye startled him.

Although he turned his head quickly toward the light, it left as quickly as it came. He stood up and looked around, but there was nothing there. When he went back to the chair to pick up the lollipop, it had changed. He examined it closely and he realized it was no longer made of wood like he made it, but a real lollipop that was colored red and smelled like cherry! Stunned, he took the knife and quickly carved a donut. Moments later that became real, too. He ran around the tent in circles trying to think of something else to make that wasn't food. Just then he heard someone calling his name outside the tent and ran to see who it could be.

CHAPTER 4

Bradley blinked back the sun in his eyes as he stared out of the tent he was standing in. A big man in a red shirt and blue pants was moving swiftly towards him. As the man got closer, Bradley saw he had a turned up nose and pointed ears. He also had a soft grey beard and reminded Bradley of a very large elf.

"Oh. There you are!" the man chuckled. "You must be Bradley!"

Bradley nodded hesitantly, unsure of the stranger.

"I'm Ray. Max sent me to you. I've come to take you home!" Ray laughed heartily.

"Don't just stand there. Come on!"

So they gathered the camp supplies together and headed down the mountain in a joyful trot.

Bradley was careful not to mention the Sprite or knife to Ray on the way home and when they reached his Aunt's trailer, they cheerfully parted ways. Bradley didn't mention the Sprite to his Aunt, either, and after he quickly choked down the chicken pot pie his Aunt had made him for dinner, he rushed out back to the shed they used to store lawn equipment. Looking around cautiously, he closed the shed door.

It was time to put the knife to the test. He grabbed a large chunk of wood from the wood pile next to the shed wall and began to carve. He labored most of the afternoon and well into the evening until he was satisfied with what he had done. He always wanted a dog and now it looked as though he would have one!

And he did. But when the dog came to life, he realized his carving skills needed a little work, because one of its ears was longer than the other and one eye bigger. The body was a little too small for the head and its tail also a little too long. Its right front leg was slightly shorter than the other three legs and its mouth much smaller than its nose. It was a dog just the same and he proudly named him Bark.

Over the course of the next several days, Bradley made many similar trips to the shed. He carved many other things he wanted and one day he decided it was time. He left a note for his Aunt and carrying his belongings on his back with Bark at his side, he headed down the road. He was finally going to have a place of his own.

CHAPTER 5

Bradley and Bark traveled a great distance from desert valleys to rolling hills. They came upon a small farming village that was made up of a number of cottages painted pretty pinks and blues, and the road turned to a beautiful cobblestone. But despite the delightful appearance of the town, the townspeople seemed unhappy as they suspiciously eyed Bradley and Bark as they walked through the center of town. The people frowned at them from their porch swings and colorful gardens while Bradley kept his distance and looked straight ahead. Avoiding their distrusting stares, Bradley and Bark continued on until they reached a grassy field that stretched out just beyond the edge of town. Bradley looked at Bark and they nodded to each other in agreement.

Bradley set his pack down and carefully removed a small wooden house he had carved. He etched in the bottom of it XXXL with his knife and set it down. He and Bark quickly backed away from it and suddenly the house began to bang and groan, thrusting upward until it was the size of a real house!

Delighted with his new home, Bradley set out his carved furnishings excitedly, and they grew in size as well. As he was placing some things on his bed, he heard a knock on his front door. A little nervous, he opened the door and two men were standing before him with their arms folded across their chests. The larger of the two men introduced himself as the town's Sheriff and the smaller man as the town's City Councilman.

Looking around Sam, the City Councilman exclaimed, "My! You didn't waste any time did you?"

Bradley looked worried, but didn't say anything.

But Sam pressed further, "How'd you build your house so fast?"

Bradley looked downward away from Sam and rubbed his arms, "Um. I had it delivered."

"You had it delivered?" Sam echoed, "By whom?"

"By whom?" Bradley repeated.

"Yes. That's right," Sam said, "I asked you by whom?"

"Oh! By whom, um, by those wonderful people who deliver houses," Bradley told him.

The councilman looked Bradley up and down and then a smile slowly took over the councilman's face. "Why, that's remarkable! What a great idea! That would do wonders for our town! What's their name? And where can I find them?"

Bradley looked around for a moment. "Oh, they went out of business," Bradley said uneasily.

"They did?" Sam gasped. "When did they go out of business?"

"Um, just now," Bradley informed him.

"They went out of business just now?!" Sam repeated loudly moving backward in disbelief.

"We're here to inform you," Sheriff Joe suddenly interrupted, "That you are on County land and we would like to know if you are claiming it."

"You mean I can have it?" Bradley exclaimed.

"Well, that's what we've come to find out," the councilman joined in.

"Yes. You can have it," the Sheriff continued, "for a price."

"You see Mr. Bradley, our land hasn't been producing crops like it should and we sure could use the money," the councilman whimpered.

"What my friend is asking," the Sheriff said impatiently, "is how much you willing to pay for it?"

Bradley responded by telling them he was going to end world hunger starting with their small town. Everything he grew, he would give to the town for free!

The Sheriff looked doubtful, but he and the councilman eventually agreed to Bradley's terms. They walked out of Bradley's new home occasionally glancing back at him and whispering to each other.

CHAPTER 6

That night, Bradley stayed up late trying to come up with an idea of something he could carve into life that he could feed the whole town with. For some reason, he kept remembering the fruit in his dream the night that he met the Sprite and found the knife. He decided to make one from memory the best he could. It took him a while, but he was able to duplicate one that looked like what he remembered almost exactly. And then within moments it had turned into a real fruit. But, what was it?

Hiding it in his coat the next day, he secretly took it to the town's general store believing that the merchant there might be able to tell him what it was.

Arriving at the store, he learned that the store's only employee was a man named Zack. He appeared a little cross. When Bradley handed him the fruit, Zack looked over Bradley sternly. He pulled an eye glass from a small dark blue pouch and placed it in his right eye.

"Looks like passion fruit," the man told him after a short pause. But then after shaking the piece of fruit a few minutes, he placed it gently on the counter and then leaned back, frowning.

"Doesn't seem to have any seeds," Zack announced, looking perplexed.

"Doesn't have any seeds?" Bradley asked, realizing he couldn't have carved the seeds inside the fruit.

"That's right. It's perfectly seedless," Zack confirmed.

Quickly snatching the fruit from the counter, Bradley over his shoulder thanked Zack for his help as he was leaving, and hurried back to his home.

CHAPTER 7

Bradley had to think. If he had to make each individual seed for the passion fruit, it would take him way too long. So he tried an experiment. He tried making just the vine the fruit grew on and found if he carved the passion fruit's vine and planted it, he had more passion fruit in a shorter amount of time than he would if he tried to make each one separately. So that's what he did.

But farming was a little more complicated than he thought and one of his neighbors told him he needed to get a tractor and plow. So secretly he carved a plow first. That turned out nicely, but when he made the tractor, he thought tractors only had three wheels, a small wheel in the front and two big ones in the back. People would actually stop at the edge of his field while he worked and point at his unusual farming equipment. Bradley would jiggle by them on his unsteady tractor and wave.

Some of the other farmers began using creative methods to fix their broken equipment and used Bradley's different ways to arrange their fields. One farmer used a horse saddle for the seat on his tractor. Another used a bridle bit for a step to get in his large truck. It seemed like the townspeople in general dealt with things with a more positive attitude.

And then one day as Bradley was planting his vines, he heard a thudding noise and stopped to see where it was coming from. He quickly got to his feet when he realized a horse was racing toward a cliff that overlooked Tiger Tooth Canyon. Running quickly between the cliff and the horse, Bradley waved his arms frantically and shouted at the horse to stop. The horse saw Bradley before it got close to the canyon's edge and began to rear.

After it calmed down for a moment, it turned around and headed back the way it came. The horse's owner came up to it slowly, talking to it softly and then he gently placed a rope on the horse's neck.

"I can't thank you enough, friend," the man with the horse told Bradley. And he put his hand out so he could shake Bradley's hand. Bradley put his hand out in return.

"I'm Mack," the man said as they greeted each other. "Well, actually, they call me Farmer Mack. And you are?"

"I'm Farmer Bradley," Bradley told him proudly.

"Well, how do you do, Farmer Bradley?" replied Farmer Mack still shaking Bradley's hand and smiling.

CHAPTER 8

Bradley's farming and feeding the town was successful for the most part. That is there was plenty of fruit for everyone to eat with some left over. The only problem was that people complained after eating the fruit, that they still felt hungry. Bradley started to try to find another way to make the fruit larger.

But it was nice to have someone he considered to be a good friend. It wasn't unusual for Farmer Mack and Farmer Bradley to chat with each other when they stopped their work for a break or at the end of the day when the sun set in the sky. On one such day, Farmer Mack unexpectedly remarked about Bark, Bradley's dog.

"Funny," he said, "But I know your dog's name is Bark, but I never heard him actually bark. You know, come to think of it, I haven't heard him make a sound at all."

"That's because he's shy," countered Bradley.

"He's shy?" Farmer Mack replied.

"Yes. He's very shy," Bradley insisted.

"Hmmm. Sure stands a lot, too," Farmer Mack observed.

"He's shy and alert. You know, the quiet, alert kind," Bradley told him, and started to feel guilty.

"Quiet, alert kind," Farmer Mack repeated, but looked a little doubtful.

Bradley wasn't sure if he should tell Farmer Mack the truth. He felt he could probably trust him.

"Well, I better be going," Farmer Mack told Bradley and turned towards his farm and walked away.

"Wait," Bradley blurted. But Farmer Mack didn't hear him.

CHAPTER 9

Growing concerned, Bradley lifted up one of his newer passion fruits from where it rested on the vine and measured it with a measuring tape. Even though he had made the vines bigger, the passion fruits themselves were still no larger. And the Sheriff was getting more and more persistent about what he was going to do about the passion fruits leaving everyone hungry.

Looking over his field in frustration, Bradley noticed a man walking towards him down the row of vines he was standing in.

"Can I help you?" Bradley asked the man when he got close enough to hear Bradley.

"I guess I should ask can I help you?" the man answered, dimples forming on his cheeks as he smiled.

Bradley felt annoyed.

Reading Bradley's face, the man quickly added, "Forgive me, sir, and allow me to introduce myself. I'm A. J. Hudgins and I would like to buy your plantation."

"You want to buy my what?" Bradley asked him, looking more annoyed.

"You know, your plan.... your crops," the man said, stretching out his hand over Bradley's field like a magician waving a hand over a magic trick.

"Oh, that," Bradley said, not liking the man, "I can't sell it."

"But why?" the man responded.

"Because it's not real passion fruit," Bradley told him without thinking.

"It's not real?" the man questioned with a frown.

"It's not real-ly that good," Bradley quickly corrected himself.

"Nonsense," A. J. Hudgins assured Bradley. "We have all tasted it."

"It's just they're a little woody," Bradley corrected the man.

"They're woody?" the man said, widening his eyes.

"Yes. They need a lot of treatment. Uh.., not worth all the trouble they bring," Bradley told him.

"Well, if you reconsider, here is where you can reach me," A. J. Hudgins said with a smile. "Please don't hesitate to call." He handed Bradley a small business card and looked at him thoughtfully for a second.

"Oh. I will, um, I mean I won't," Bradley replied.

As A. J. Hudgins walked away, Bradley could hear him mutter under his breath, "He is one unusual boy, that one." And the man shook his head as he made his way back across the field where he came from.

CHAPTER 10

Bradley stayed up later and later every night, but still found no solution to the problem with his passion fruit. Sleeping past the normal waking hours for a good farmer, Bradley's sleep was interrupted by a loud knock on his door.

"Mr. Bradley," he heard the familiar voice of the councilman say, "We need to talk to you."

"We...?" Bradley muttered, "That can't be good." And he rushed to put his clothes on.

Bradley opened the door and with a shaky voice, Bradley invited the Sheriff and City Councilman to come in.

"I'll get right to the point," the Sheriff started, but paused as if something made him forget what he was going to say.

"That's a very suitable amount of wood you got piled there," the Sheriff noted after a moment as he looked at Bradley's firewood pile in the hallway by his back door. Then his eyes turned to the chimney Bradley made. Bradley had forgotten to make an opening to put the wood in.

"But where do you put it?" the Sheriff continued.

When Bark entered the room, Bradley was thankful for the distraction.

"Come here, fella," the councilman said as leaned down towards Bark. "Does he bite?" he asked.

"Oh no, he can't. I forgot to give him teeth," Bradley assured him.

"You forgot to...," the councilman stammered raising an eyebrow.

"I mean, I forgot he has no teeth," Bradley quickly added.

"NO teeth? ALL his teeth?" the councilman moaned. "How did he lose all his teeth?"

"Hum..., I'm not quite sure," Bradley told him.

"Your dog lost all his teeth and you aren't sure how?" said the councilman.

"I guess I forgot that, too," Bradley replied sheepishly.

"We spoke with A. J. Hudgins, Bradley," the Sheriff cut in, "And he's prepared to pay us money for the land you're on. You have exactly 24 hours to live up to your end of our bargain and feed the people of this town with something that actually makes them full or we're going to sell your property, house and all, to A. J. Hudgins! Good day!"

"Uh," the councilman stuttered hurrying behind the Sheriff as he marched toward the front door, "We can see our way out."

The two men left, slamming the door behind them.

CHAPTER 11

Bradley had spent all that night and early into the next morning carving passion fruit in different ways, but nothing made them good enough to eat. His spirits low and his wood pile even lower, he stopped for a moment to think. As he turned towards the clock on the wall to see how much time he had left, there suddenly appeared next to his right eye a flicker of light. Excited, he jumped up, dropping his knife on the ground. He lunged forward towards the direction he thought the light had taken and stepped down hard on the knife. With a loud snap, it broke in two.

Then, everything in the room that he made began to turn to wood and he quickly ran out of the house. Once outside, he could hear the people in town as they ran from their houses, and shouted about passion fruit and wood. Not knowing what to do, Bradley started running toward them, but then realized a crowd had formed and it was moving quickly in his direction. He turned back around and started running to what used to be his house, but was now a small piece of wood with the letters XXXL scribbled on it. Looking back at the angry voices, he saw the mob was getting closer with the Sheriff and the City Councilman leading them. In the very front of the two of them was A. J. Hudgins!

He ran harder and saw Bark following him for a short distance trying to keep up, but the dog slowed to a halt as he turned back to wood. Leaving Bark behind, Bradley ran past the stream that trickled near his house. He headed for Tiger Tooth Canyon, but was cut off when he reached the edge of the ravine.

Bradley prepared to jump off the cliff, but a hand grabbed him by the back of the shirt and threw him into the back of a wagon. The horse pulling it started running as fast as it could. Looking around, he realized it was Farmer Mack's wagon. He bumped up and down as the wagon bounced out of town with him safely inside.

Chapter 12

Farmer Mack quickly ushered Bradley into his barn and made sure no one was following. Up in the loft, he prepared a soft bed for Bradley out of straw. They sat together and talked the rest of the day until they both felt tired. Bradley finally shared with him what had happened with the Sprite and knife. Farmer Mack never said if he believed him or not, but told Bradley he knew he was a hard worker and offered him a job as a farm hand on his farm. Bradley eagerly accepted.

And then one day after Bradley returned from his chores, Farmer Mack called him into the main farm house to have a talk with him. Bradley a little alarmed, trusted Farmer Mack and entered the large country kitchen where he was told to have a seat. Farmer Mack came in a different door and seemed to be struggling with an object of some kind. Looking confused, Bradley asked if he could help.

"I think you can," Farmer Mack declared. With that he was in the room and there at his side was a dog that Bradley had never seen before.

"If you think you can take care of him, you can have him," Farmer Mack offered.

Eyeing the dog carefully, Bradley noticed he only had one eye and his one front leg didn't straighten all the way, making it appear shorter than the others.

"I was out plowing the back field when I found him by the roadside injured and scared. I think he was hit by a car. I thought I'd bring him home and see what we could do," the caring farmer explained.

"It's Bark!!!" Bradley suddenly cried loudly.

With that the dog wagged his tail and barked back at Bradley two times. The dog then limped over to Bradley. Bradley knelt down to hug him and buried his face deep within Bark's warm, thick fur.

"Thank you so much!" Bradley said as he choked back grateful tears.

Things got much better for Bradley. By this time, the people in town had forgotten about passion fruit, because Bradley would always lend a helping hand to anyone who needed one when he was there.

"That Bradley sure is helpful," the townsfolk would say to each other, "And thoughtful, too."

The high prices that A.J. Hudgins charged for his sugar beets gave everyone something to complain about and that helped keep their minds off of Bradley, too.

CHAPTER 13

Living on a farm, Bradley found he preferred farm life over cooking for miners. He liked the feel of working under the open blue sky compared to being cooped up in a ragged old tent all day. He loved the sounds of the sheep baaing loudly off in the distance and the sight of geese forming a V shape over his head while traveling to a better climate. But mostly, he liked spending time with Bark and Farmer Mack.

One day, after plowing the fields, Bradley stopped his tractor and got off. He climbed up the green hillside to the top of Bark boulder (or so Bradley called it), because Bark would lie there patiently all day waiting for Bradley to finish his work and come join him. Bradley was happy too, because from the top of the boulder you could see everywhere. Today, he looked carefully over the fields he just plowed. Bradley then relaxed and breathed in deeply as he laid one hand on Bark next to him. Satisfied with the formation of the fields and the pinkish sunset, Bradley thoughtfully stroked Bark's soft fur.

In a hushed voice, that he made sure only Bark could hear, he whispered, "I do have everything, you know. I didn't need magic. I had it all along. And I have everything that matters."

Off in the distance Bradley and Bark could hear the clang of the farm house dinner bell calling them in for the night. It felt good, at last, to be home.

Acknowledgements

A special thanks to Patricia Mahoney for all her help with editing this book. I definitely couldn't have done it without you. I also want to thank my children and beautiful grandchildren for sharing their wishes with me and for all their input. I want you all to know, you are everything to me.

CPSIA information can be obtained
at www.ICGtesting.com
Printed in the USA
BVHW031644200120
569976BV00005B/18/J